D0521977

Peronnik
the Simpleton

A Breton folk-tale
Illustrated by Christiane Lesch

Floris Books

First published in German as Peronnik © *1984 Verlag Freies Geistesleben GmbH Stuttgart*
This translation is abridged from Breton Folktales © *1971 G Bell & Sons Ltd*
This edition © Floris Books, 21 Napier Road, Edinburgh, 1984
Printed in Belgium by Offset Printing Van den Bossche.
ISBN 0-86315-018-7

No doubt you have come across one of those poor simple souls, who are like calves that have lost the way back to the byre. With big eyes and open mouth, they look around, as if they were searching for something, but the thing they are looking for is not so common in this country that you will find it lying in the road: it is common sense we are talking of.

Peronnik was one of those poor wretches. He always followed his nose, and did not know whither. If he felt thirst he drank from a spring, and if he felt hunger he begged crusts from the women on their doorsteps. When sleep came upon him he found himself a hayrick and burrowed in it like a lizard, and whenever he had had enough to eat, Peronnik sang with all his heart, thanking God morning and night for giving him so many gifts when he was under no obligation to do so.

Peronnik had never learned any trade, but he was handy in many ways. He ate as much as was asked of him, he slept longer than any-one else, and he imitated the song of the lark with his tongue. There are quite a few people nowadays who certainly cannot equal that.

At that time I am speaking of, a thousand and more years ago, the land of the white corn was not the same as it is now. One day Peronnik came to a farm that stood on the edge of the forest of Paimpont.

The farmer's wife was kneeling on the doorstep, using her brimstone to clean the porridge pan; but when she heard the voice of the simpleton asking for food in the name of the true Lord, she stopped and held the pan up to him.

"Take it," she said, "my poor simpleton, eat the scrapings and in return you can say an Our Father for our piglets which are not thriving."

Peronnik sat down on the ground, took the pan between his legs and started to scrape it with his nails; but there was little to be got, for every spoon in the house had already been round it. But he licked his fingers and gave a satisfied grunt, as if he had never had better fare before.

"It is millet-flour," he said half to himself, "millet-flour with milk from a black cow, and stirred by the best cook in all Brittany."

The farmer's wife, who had already turned away, turned back again flattered.

"Poor simpleton," she said, "there is only a little left, but I shall give you some black bread as well."

She brought the lad a slice cut from a loaf that had just come from the oven. Peronnik bit into it like a wolf into a leg of lamb and called out that the dough had surely been kneaded by his Lordship the Bishop of Vannes' personal baker.

Proudly the farmer's wife replied that it would be quite another thing again if the bread were spread with freshly churned butter, and to prove it she brought a little butter in a small covered dish.

Peronnik extolled each piece more than the last and, whilst he was thus employed building up his strength, an armed knight appeared by the door of the house, addressed the woman and asked her the way to Castle Kerglas.

"Jesus, oh Lord, Sir Knight! Is that where you want to go?" the farmer's wife exclaimed.

"Yes," replied the warrior, "for that I have come from a country so far away that I had to ride day and night for three months to get here."

"And what do you seek in Kerglas?" the Breton wife now asked him.

"I am looking for the golden bowl and the adamantine lance," replied the knight. "For apart from the bowl producing all the food and riches one desires, it is enough just to drink from it to be healed from all ills, and even the dead rise again if it touches their lips. But the adamantine lance kills and destroys everything it touches."

"And who owns this lance and this bowl?" Peronnik said wonderingly.

"A sorcerer called Rogéar who lives in the castle of Kerglas," the farmer's wife replied; "every day you can see him riding past, along the edge of the forest, on a black mare, followed by a foal thirteen months old; but none would dare to attack him, for in his hand he holds the cruel lance. You, too, will not succeed, Sir. More than a hundred other nobles have tried the venture before you, but not one of them has returned."

"That I know, good woman," the knight replied, "but they did not have the advice of the Hermit of Blavet beforehand, as I did."

"And what did this hermit tell you?" Peronnik asked him.

"He has told me everything I must do," answered the stranger; "first I must ride through the trackless forest, where all kinds of sorcery will be tried to frighten me and keep me from the right way. When I have passed through it, I shall meet a dwarf armed with a fiery goad. Everything he touches with it is turned to ashes. This dwarf guards an apple tree, and from this tree I must pluck a fruit."

"And then?" Peronnik wanted to know.

"Then I shall find the laughing flower which is guarded by a lion with a mane of serpents. This flower I must pluck. Then I must cross the dragon lake, and fight the black man with the iron ball which always reaches its goal and returns to its master of its own accord. Finally I shall enter the valley of pleasures where I shall see everything that can tempt a man and hold him back, and I shall come to a river that has only one ford. There I shall find a lady dressed in black; I take her behind me on my horse and she will tell me what I must do next."

The farmer's wife tried to convince the stranger that he would never pass the seven tests; but he spurred his horse and disappeared among the trees.

The farmer's wife sighed deeply.

Peronnik was just about to be on his way when the farmer returned from the fields. He had chased away the boy who minded his cows on the edge of the forest and was now wondering how he would find another. Seeing the simpleton was like a ray of light to him; he thought he had found what he was looking for, and after talking of this and that he asked Peronnik straight out if he would stay at the farm and mind the cows.

Peronnik would have preferred just minding himself, for none was better at doing nothing but he; but he still had the taste of the bacon on his tongue, and of the fresh butter, the black bread and the millet porridge; so he followed these inducements and accepted the farmer's offer.

The man immediately took him to the edge of the forest, counted out aloud every cow to him, not forgetting the heifers, and cut him a hazel switch, to help him keep them together; then he told him to drive the cattle home at sundown.

And so Peronnik became a cowherd; he had to stop the cows from doing damage, and had to run from the black cow to the red, and from the red to the white, to keep them together properly.

Whilst he was thus running from one cow to the other he heard the sound of horses' hooves and became aware of the sorcerer Rogéar on a forest track, sitting on his mare, followed by the foal thirteen months old. Around his neck he wore the golden bowl and in his hand was the adamantine lance that shone like a flame.

Peronnik was frightened and hid behind a bush; the giant went by quite close to him and continued on his way. When he had disappeared Peronnik left his hiding place and looked in the direction which the sorcerer had taken, yet he could not make out which way he had gone.

Now armed knights were coming all the time, looking for Castle Kerglas, but none was ever seen to return. And the giant went for his ride each day.

The simpleton, gradually growing more daring, no longer hid when he went past, and observed him from afar with envious eyes, for the desire to own the golden bowl and the adamantine lance grew stronger in his heart day by day.

Peronnik knew now that if one wanted to go to Kerglas the first thing was to catch the foal who knew the way.

Peronnik pondered for a long time on this and finally it seemed to him that he might succeed. The simpleton could not hope to stand up to the giant, and so he decided to use cunning instead. He did not shrink from the difficulties, for he knew that medlars are as hard as pebbles when one picks them, but with a little straw and much patience they will get soft in the end.

And so he made all his preparations for the hour when the giant would appear at the edge of the forest. First of all he made a halter and a fetter from black hemp, then a snare for catching snipe, dipping the hair he used into holy water, a linen bag which he filled with bird lime and larks' feathers, a rosary, a whistle cut from an elder branch, and a crust of bread rubbed with rancid bacon. Next he made a trail with the crumbs of the piece of bread he had been given for his lunch, along the road which Rogéar must take with his mare and the foal thirteen months old.

All three appeared at the usual hour and crossed the meadow as they did every day; but the foal, walking along sniffing the road with its head hanging down, smelled the bread and stopped to eat it, so that soon it was left behind, out of sight of the giant.

Now Peronnik crept up to it, quickly put the halter on, fettered two of its legs with the ropes, jumped on its back and let it go where it would, for he was sure that the foal, knowing the way, would take him to Castle Kerglas.

And indeed the little horse did not hesitate and took one of the wildest tracks, running as fast as the fetters would let it. Peronnik trembled like a leaf, for all the magic of the forest was combined to frighten him. Now it seemed that an abyss opened wide before his mount, then the trees appeared to be in flames and he felt himself to be in the midst of a great fire; often, when he was crossing a stream, the stream would change to a raging river, threatening to carry him away; another time, when the path followed the foot of a hill, enormous masses of rocks would break off and come hurtling down to smash him. However often the simpleton reminded himself that these things were only illusions created by the sorcerer, still the blood froze in his veins with fear. Finally he pulled his cap right over his eyes, so that he would see no more, and let the foal carry him along.

Then they reached a plain where the sorcery came to an end. Peronnik took off his cap and looked around. It was a dry heath, more dismal than a churchyard. From time to time one came across the skeletons of the knights who had gone to look for Castle Kerglas. There they lay, stretched out beside their horses, and grey wolves were gnawing at their bones.

Finally the simpleton came to a meadow that was completely overshadowed by a single apple tree. This tree was so loaded with fruit that the branches bent right down to the ground. Before the tree stood a dwarf, and in his hand he held the fiery weapon that changed everything it touched to ashes. When he saw Peronnik he cawed like a cormorant and raised his weapon; but the young man did not show the least surprise and politely raised his cap.

"Do not let me disturb you, little sir," he said, "I only want to pass to get to Castle Kerglas. The sorcerer Rogéar has asked me to come."

"You?" the dwarf replied. "But who are you?"

"I am the master's new servant," the simpleton answered, "you know — the one he is waiting for."

"I do not know of anything," said the dwarf, "and you look just like a trickster to me."

"Excuse me," Peronnik interrupted him, "that is not my profession, I am merely a bird catcher and bird trainer."

But the dwarf still seemed in doubt and asked him why the sorcerer needed a bird catcher.

"He needs one urgently, it appears," Peronnik replied, "for he says everything that grows in the gardens of Kerglas is being eaten by birds at the moment."

"And how are you going to stop them?" the dwarf asked.

Peronnik showed the little snare he had made and said no bird could escape it.

"I would like to make sure of that," the dwarf decided. "Blackbirds and thrushes are also plundering my apple tree; set up your snare, and if you can catch them I shall let you pass."

Peronnik agreed; he bound his foal to a tree and approached the trunk of the apple tree. He tied one end of the snare to it and then called to the dwarf to hold the other whilst he put up the lures. The dwarf did what the simpleton asked of him; and Peronnik suddenly pulled the slip-knot fast, and the dwarf was caught, just like a bird. He screeched with fury and tried to free himself, but the snare, having been dipped in holy water, resisted all his attempts. The simpleton had time to go up to the tree, pick an apple, and then get on his foal again and continue on his way.

So they left the plain and saw before them some pleasure gardens, with the most beautiful plants growing in them. There were roses of all colours, Spanish gorse, red honeysuckle, and above them all rose a fairy flower that was laughing; but a lion with a mane of serpents was running round the garden, rolling his eyes and gnashing his teeth like two freshly ground millstones.

Peronnik stopped and greeted him, too, for he knew well that before the mighty in the land the place of a cap is not on the head, but in the hand. He expressed all the good wishes he could think of for the lion and his family, and at length, in an off-hand way, asked if he was on the right way for Kerglas.

"And what do you want in Kerglas?" roared the wild animal, looking most ferocious.

"With your permission," the simpleton replied anxiously, "I am in the service of a lady who is a friend of Sir Rogéar, and she is sending him a present, to make a lark pie with."

"Larks?" the lion repeated and passed his tongue over his whiskers. "It has been a century since I last had any. Do you have many of them?"

"As many as this bag will hold, your lordship," Peronnik replied, holding up the linen bag which he had filled with feathers and bird-lime. And to make his words bear more weight he began to imitate the twittering of larks.

This song increased the lion's appetite.

"Let me see," he said and came closer. "Show me your birds, I want to be sure they are fat enough to be served up for the master."

"I should like to do that," the simpleton replied, "but I fear that they may fly away if I take them out of the bag."

"Only open it so far," said the wild animal, "that I may look in."

This was what Peronnik had hoped for; he held the linen bag out to the lion who put his head in it, hoping to get the larks, but found himself instead held fast among the feathers and the bird-lime. The simpleton quickly pulled the cord of the bag tight round his neck, made the sign of the cross over the knot, that it might never open, and ran to the laughing flower, picked it and hurried away as fast as his foal would carry him.

Soon, however, he came to the dragon lake. He had to swim across it, and as soon as he was in the water, dragons came hurrying up from all sides to devour him.

This time Peronnik did not stop to doff his cap, but threw the pearls of the rosary to them, much as one throws corn to the ducks, and each time a pearl was swallowed a dragon turned over on his back and was dead, so that the simpleton was able to reach the other shore unharmed.

There remained the valley guarded by the black man. Peronnik saw him, right at the entrance, his feet fettered to the rock and in his hand the iron ball which, having reached its goal, would always return to him of its own accord. He had six eyes right round his head, which kept watch in turn, but at the moment all of them were open.

Peronnik knew that as soon as he was noticed, the iron ball would strike him, before he could even say a word; he therefore preferred to creep along behind the undergrowth. Hidden by the bushes he came within a few paces of the man; he was just sitting down, and two of his eyes were closed in sleep.

Peronnik thought he might be tired, and began to sing the first part of Mass in a low voice. The black man seemed surprised at first, and turned his head, but the song had its effect, and the third eye closed. Peronnik now intoned the *Kyrie eleison*, and the black man closed his fourth eye, and half the fifth. Peronnik started on the Vespers, but before he reached the *Magnificat*, the black man had fallen asleep.

The boy took the foal by the rein and led it quietly over moss-covered spots; and quickly passing by the watchman he arrived in the valley of pleasures.

That was the most difficult test of all, for here it was not a question of escaping danger, but of resisting temptation. Peronnik called on all the saints of Brittany for help.

The valley through which he was passing was like a garden full of fruit, flowers and springs: but wine and sweet, intoxicating drinks flowed from the springs; the flowers sang with voices as pure as the cherubim in paradise, and the fruit offered itself of its own accord. At every turn of the road Peronnik saw great tables covered with food fit for kings; and just a little further away beautiful young girls were rising from the bath and dancing in the meadow; they called him by name and asked him to lead the dance. The simpleton did make the sign of the cross, but without noticing it he was riding more slowly on his foal; he lifted his nose into the wind, that he might sniff the smell from the dishes all the better, and see the bathing girls. His foal almost stopped, and that would have been the end of Peronnik; but then the thought of the golden bowl and the adamantine lance flashed through his mind.

Right away Peronnik started to play on his elder-branch whistle, that he might no longer hear the inviting voices; he ate his crust of bread rubbed in rancid bacon to overcome the smell from the rich dishes, and he looked at the ears of the horse, so that he might no longer see the dancers.

In this way he reached the end of the garden without mishap and at last saw Castle Kerglas lie before him.

But he was still separated from it by the river he had been told about, which had only one ford. Fortunately the foal knew it and entered the water at the right place.

Now Peronnik looked around him to try and find the lady who was to take him to the castle, and he saw her sitting on a rock. She was clothed in black silk, and her face was as yellow as that of a Moorish lady. The simpleton doffed his cap and asked her if she did not want to cross the river.

"That is why I am waiting for you," replied the lady, "come closer, that I may get on behind you."

Peronnik rode closer, let her get up behind him and started to ride across the ford.

In the middle of the river the lady said to him: "And do you know who I am, my poor boy?"

"Forgive me," answered Peronnik, "but to judge from your clothes you must be a noble and powerful lady."

"Noble I must be, no doubt, for my race goes back to the original Fall of man; and powerful I am, too, for all the peoples on earth bow down before me."

"And what is your name, gracious lady, if I may ask?" Peronnik asked.

"I am called the Plague!" the yellow woman replied.

The simpleton leapt on his horse and was about to throw himself in the river, but the Plague said to him: "Stay where you are, poor boy, you need not fear me, and I might even be able to do you a service."

"Is it possible, that you would be so gracious, Dame Plague?" Peronnik said, this time doffing his cap and not putting it on again. "Ah yes, now I remember that you were to tell me how I could rid myself of the sorcerer Rogéar."

"The sorcerer must die," said the yellow lady.

"Nothing would suit me better," replied Peronnik, "but he is immortal."

"Listen and try to understand," the lady said. "The apple tree guarded by the dwarf grew from a cutting of the Tree of Good and Evil planted by God himself in the earthly paradise. Its fruit, like that of which Adam and Eve once ate, makes immortals subject to death. See to it that the sorcerer eats the apple. Tell him, his brother Bryak has sent you with the apple. Then I need only touch him and he will live no longer."

"I shall try," said Peronnik. "But if I succeed, how can I get hold of the golden bowl and the adamantine lance? They lie hidden in a dark dungeon that will open to no key forged by man."

"The laughing flower opens all doors and lights up all darkness," the Plague replied.

After this they reached the other shore and the simpleton went towards the castle.

In front of the gate was a big sheltering roof, like the canopy under which his Lordship the Bishop of Vannes walks in the procession of the holy sacrament. Here the giant sprawled, his legs crossed like those of a farmer who has got in his harvest, smoking a tobacco-pipe of pure gold.

When he saw the foal with Peronnik and the yellow lady in black silk on its back, he raised his head and said in a voice rolling like thunder: "By Beelzebub, our master! That is my foal of thirteen months which that stupid boy is riding."

"So it is, O greatest of all sorcerers!" Peronnik replied.

"And how did you manage to get hold of it?" Rogéar asked.

"I repeated the words which your brother Bryak taught me," the simpleton replied. "And the little creature came at once."

"So you know my brother?" the giant asked.

"As one knows one's master," the boy replied.

"And why is he sending you?"

"To bring you two rare things which he has just received from the Moorish lands: this apple of joy here, and the submissive woman there, whom you see before you. If you eat the apple you will be for ever contented, like the poor man who has found a bag with a hundred pieces of gold in a wooden shoe; and if you take the woman into your service, there will be nothing left for you to desire on this earth."

"Give me the apple then, and let the Moorish woman get down."

Oh, how quickly the simpleton obeyed; but as soon as the giant had bitten into the fruit the yellow lady touched him and he dropped to the ground like an ox that has been struck by lightning.

Peronnik immediately entered the castle, in his hand the laughing flower. He hurried through more than fifty halls one opening into the other, and finally reached the vault with the silver gate. This opened of its own accord to the flower, and the flower lit up the darkness for the simpleton and made it possible for him to get to the golden bowl and the adamantine lance. Hardly had he taken hold of them, however, when the ground shook under his feet and there were terrible crashing noises, the palace disappeared, and Peronnik found himself in the middle of a clearing in the forest.

With his two magic objects he went to the court of the King of Brittany. But as he passed through Vannes he took care to buy himself the richest clothes he could find, and the best horse that was for sale in the cathedral town of the land of white corn.

When he reached Nantes, this city was just being besieged by an enemy. They had laid waste to all the fields around, leaving hardly a tree on which a goat might find anything to nibble. People were starving in the city, and any soldiers who did not die of their wounds perished from lack of bread.

The very day when Peronnik arrived, therefore, a trumpeter announced at every street corner that the King of Brittany would make anyone who could liberate the city and drive away the enemy his heir.

When the simpleton heard this promise, he said to the trumpeter: "Do not call out any longer, but take me to the King. I can do what he wants to be done."

"You?" said the trumpeter, seeing how young and how small he was. "Get away with you, you little goldfinch, the King does not have time for catching birds."

Instead of a reply Peronnik touched the soldier with his lance, making him drop dead to the ground the same moment, to the horror of the people who stood watching and now tried to escape. But Peronnik called out: "You have seen what I can do to my enemies, now come and see what I can do for my friends!"

He put the magic bowl to the lips of the dead man, who immediately returned to life.

When the King heard of this miracle he put Peronnik in command of the soldiers still left to him; the simpleton used his lance to kill thousands of the enemy, and his bowl to bring all the dead Bretons back to life; and so he drove away the enemy armies in a few days, winning all the booty they left behind them in their camp.

Finally, when he had done all this for the King, he declared that he wished to go and free the Holy Land, and took ship at Nantes, in big vessels, together with all the greatest nobles of the land.

Some say that thanks to the golden bowl he and his sons live still, ruling this country. Others assure us that Rogéar's brother, the sorcerer Bryak, got hold of the two magic objects again, and that those who want them will only have to look for them . . .